# SCI FI SEX STORIES

## EXPLICIT DIRTY EROTICA SHORT STORIES

HELANA PARKINS

plicit Press
Erotica Fiction

# CHAPTER 1

## MORE THAN A WOMAN

ADAM WALKER SR. invented the fuckdoll in 2056. Not a blow-up doll or something that looked like a machine. No, he designed a full-on android whose only desire was to please his or her master. When he died thirteen years later, he was filthy rich and estranged from his only child. Adam Jr., or AJ as he was known to his friends, knew he'd inherited billions, but it was the keycard to his father's lab that had intrigued him the most. What he found there changed everything.

Twenty-three-year-old AJ Walker hesitated outside the door, keycard in hand. He wasn't sure if he wanted to do this. He may have looked like his dad – unruly dark blond hair, periwinkle blue eyes, and freckles – and had a head for science, but they were as different as could be. AJ wanted to use his abilities for good, not perpetuate the growing epidemic of people who would rather fuck a machine than find a human mate.

"Can I help you?"

.  .  .

AJ turned... and stared. He was vaguely aware that his jaw was hanging open, but he didn't seem to be able to stop himself. She was about his age, medium height, and slender. Straight black hair that hung halfway down her back, intelligent pale gray/blue eyes, fair skin. She was pretty, her nose a trifle too long to be perfectly beautiful. A thin scar marred her upper lip and AJ found himself wanting to kiss it. Then her lab coat registered and he realized that she worked at the center.

"Sir?"

AJ shook his head, heat rushing to his cheeks. "I came to see my dad's office." "Oh," her eyes widened slightly, expression softening. "You're Dr. Walker's son."

AJ nodded, shifting uncomfortably. "Yeah." He turned his back on the young woman, swiping the card.

"He spoke of you often."

AJ jumped. He hadn't heard her follow him in.

"I'm Nona, by the way," she held out a hand. "I was your dad's assistant."

Later, AJ couldn't remember exactly how it happened. One minute he was shaking her hand, the next she was crying, and his arms were around her. As her tears soaked into his shirt, she was apologizing.

"He was your father, but he was always so nice to me and I don't have any family or really know a lot of people."

"Shh," AJ awkwardly patted her head, completely at a loss; then she was looking up at him, tears shining in her eyes and he was lost.

Without realizing he was going to do it, he lowered his head and covered her mouth with his. He heard her gasp of surprise and used the opportunity to slide the tip of his tongue across her bottom lip, darting inside to test her reaction. Her arms snaked around his neck and she pressed her body closer to his, opening her mouth, tongue tentatively venturing out to caress his.

AJ made a noise in the back of his throat, moving one hand up to cup the back of her head, marveling at the soft texture of her hair. His other hand slid under her coat and down her back, hesitating at her waist. When she hooked one leg around him, grinding her pelvis against him, he dropped his hand to cup her ass.

She broke the kiss, panting as she spoke. "I don't normally do this..."

"Me either," AJ searched her face as he continued. "We can stop..." Nona took a step back and he let her go, trying to hide his disappointment.

"I don't want to stop," Nona removed her lab coat and lay it over the back of a nearby chair. She gave him a half-smile that didn't quite clear the sadness from her eyes. "It just might be easier with fewer clothes."

He followed her example, placing each garment on one of the chairs. When he turned back towards her, they were both naked. Her eyes ran over him, open admiration on her face as her gaze moved from his broad shoulders, across his muscular torso, and down to his cock. It sprang to full attention as Nona's eyes darkened with lust. AJ took the opportunity as she walked towards him to do his own perusal. Her body was slender, just the barest hint of hips. The hair between her legs was sparse and dark. Her breasts were small but firm, and the nipples hardened caramel-colored pebbles.

"Nona," AJ started to speak, to give her a way out.

She placed a finger over his lips, her body just centimeters away from his. His dick brushed against her stomach. "Please, AJ, I need this."

He put his hands on her waist and lifted her onto the table. She leaned forward to capture his mouth with hers, hooking her legs around his waist and pulling him closer. His tip nudged at her entrance and AJ groaned. She sucked his tongue into her mouth as he pushed forward. She was virgin- tight and, as he inched his way into her pussy, part of him wondered if that was the case. When he came to rest, fully sheathed in her wet heat, without encountering a barrier, he knew she was just that tight.

Her cunt clung to his cock, creating the most delicious friction when he started to move.

Nona's nails raked down his back and she flung her head back, crying out as her body convulsed around him. AJ stilled, resisting the urge to thrust, wanting this to last. He lowered his head and wrapped his mouth around her breast, lips wide to take in flesh with her nipple. As he began to suck, Nona's pussy spasmed around his cock, her body racked by another orgasm.

AJ shuddered, fighting for control. She was so tight and hot around him, so responsive. He ran his fingers over her shoulders and down her arms, enjoying how the lightest touch made her shiver. His hand bumped against a glass beaker, the cool surface reminding him that they weren't in a place conducive to a leisurely encounter. He scraped his teeth over her nipple as he let it fall from his mouth, smiling when Nona swore.

"Please," she begged, nails digging into his shoulders.

He grasped her hips and began to thrust, hips snapping forward with enough force to make Nona cry out with each one. Her hands dropped from his shoulders to her breasts, her fingers closing on the small brown nubs. The sight of her tugging on her nipples, the clenching of her cunt around him, was too much and AJ came, driving himself deep inside.

They held each other for a minute, foreheads resting on each other's shoulders, breathing in each other's scent, her fresh like spring rain, him like a pine forest. Both scents mingled with that of their union. AJ's tongue darted out, flicking across Nona's skin, the salt from her sweat exploding across his taste buds.

"I should go," the reluctance was clear in Nona's voice. "I'm supposed to be distributing Professor Walker's work among his colleagues."

AJ wandered around the lab, unable to keep Nona out of his mind. They'd dressed in silence, without making plans to see each other again even though he'd desperately wanted to. He hadn't spoken up, scared that she'd say this had been a result of grief, nothing more. He'd come back, he decided, maybe next week, see where things went, see if she still wanted him.

A hologram case caught his eye. His name was written in his father's strong script. He opened it. Password requested. Intrigued, AJ put in his birthday. No luck. He sat down in front of his father's desk. A memory tugged at the back of his mind, far back when he and his father had still been on good terms. After AJ's mother had died, they'd set aside a day for the two of them to spend together, a day when even the esteemed Professor Walker would stop working. He put in the date of their last day together.

The case beeped and opened. The small holographic image of his father made AJ's heart constrict, but when the familiar voice started speaking, the information drove everything else from his mind.

"AJ, I know we've had our differences and I have no right to ask anything of you, especially now that I'm gone, but there is no one else I trust with this secret. I have been working over the years to produce more human androids, a task I know you don't approve of. About six months ago, I succeeded. I have created an android so much like a human that even she doesn't know that she is a machine.

Please care for her and, whatever you do, don't tell her what she is. I don't know how she'll react."

AJ shook his head. He didn't want to hear this. Didn't want to know what right now only suspicion was. It couldn't be true. He didn't know what he would do if it was. He couldn't still feel this way, could he? Maybe it was all a mistake. But, even as he hoped for a reprieve, he heard the four words that changed everything.

"I call her Nona."

# CHAPTER 2

## CAPTAIN MALONE'S EXTRA-TERRESTRIAL AFFAIR

"PLANET ANTHON IS about sixty kilometers away captain," First Lieutenant Rogers informed the captain of their vessel. For weeks now, they'd been searching for this mysterious planet, which was said to have extraterrestrial life.

Although the people back home on Earth believed that their mission would be unsuccessful, Captain Bruce Malone felt deep down he would find this planet. And now here they were, approaching it.

Captain Malone and his crew of twenty had been searching for this planet for years. He'd believed that there was extraterrestrial life on this planet, based on the stories that his father, former captain of the Weganda, the vessel that he was now commanding, told him. His father had even told him of his experience with an Anthonam woman named Greta. He'd met her in Providence, the small base that humans had set up on the moon.

During an attack on their planet, some of the Anthonam's had escaped to the moon. "They're the most beautiful women you'll ever meet, son," his father had told him one day while they shared a few beers together. Now years later, Captain Malone was determined to find out for himself whether the rumors were true.

They soon arrived at their destination planet, Anthon. Surprisingly, the planet seemed very much like earth. The place where they landed had lush tropical trees. As he stepped out of the spacecraft a creature in the distance caught his attention. It looked like a woman and she was calling out to him.

The captain immediately left his crew, ignoring their warnings. They were in a strange place and feared that something bad might happen to him. But anyone who knew Captain Malone well knew that he was a brave man at heart. And also very stubborn. He told them to keep looking around and searching for anything they could take back to earth, as proof. Meanwhile, he followed the woman in the distance.

When he caught up to her, he realized that she was a human being just like him; well at least that's how it appeared to be. He introduced himself to the woman. Her name was Ambiataqua. She was an Anthonam, with bright red hair, and the most beautiful green eyes, he'd ever seen. He had so many questions. And he didn't hesitate before asking her several of them.

Ambiataqua invited him to walk with her, as she answered his questions. She answered his most important question, which was why did she look so much like a human being. She told him that they were shapeshifters and they could take the shape of anything around them. They were also very intelligent beings with great eyesight.

They approached a waterfall, and before he could protest, she began kissing along his neck. "Please let me, I've always dreamed about what it felt like to make love to a human." She begged.

She had a certain charm that he could not resist. They locked lips and soon they were ripping away at each other's clothing. "Teach me how to love you, my human," she cooed, stroking his manhood with her hands.

"You're so beautiful Ambiataqua. Let me love you here, in the water." He breathed the words against her neck, nibbling her earlobe, kissing her neck. Ambiataqua sighed. Captain Malone turned her around to face her, sliding his hands down to cup her ass, pulling her against his cock, now pressed against her stomach. He rubbed himself against her a moment, kissing her deeply, his tongue probing her mouth, skating across her lips.

"Wrap your legs around my waist, Ambiataqua." He slid one hand down the back of her thigh, pulling her leg up. She ran the calf of her leg up over his hips, her foot in the small of his back. She felt his cock slide between her legs.

Captain Malone shifted his body, spreading his legs and sliding his other hand down her thigh. She wrapped her arms around his neck and slid the other leg up Captain Malone's body, crossing her ankles, and locking her legs behind him. She felt buoyant in the water; she also felt Captain Malone's cock pressing against her pussy, his fingers buried in the cleft of her ass.

With practiced ease, Captain Malone shifts his body, his cock sliding into Ambiataqua, cool from the water but soon heated from his passion. He flexed his hips up and pushed down on Ambiataqua's ass, sliding his cock into her overstimulated pussy. She was more than ready to cum; as Captain Malone started thrusting up, she felt her body respond and pick up where they'd left off on the towel.

Her wet breasts were rubbing against Captain Malone's

chest, the nipples sensitive from both arousal and the sun. A tiny voice said she was going to be in pain later, but she was enjoying the sensation of her over-heated skin rubbing against David, her nipples responding, sending jolts of pleasure straight to her pussy.

"Ah, Ambiataqua, this feels so good, you feel so good." Captain Malone breathed the words into her neck, his breath already coming in ragged gasps as he hungrily kissed her neck, nibbling on her earlobe, his tongue probing her ear. He was thrusting into her faster now, still pushing her down on his cock with his hands, his probing fingers touching every burying himself to the hilt with each powerful thrust.

Ambiataqua felt warmth pooling in the center of her stomach, moving down, and pressure building in her pussy. She snaked one hand between their bodies, finding her clit and rubbing that swollen button of flesh. She could feel the shaft of Captain Malone's cock pumping in and out of her, her fingertips brushing against him briefly. Touching herself, finally rubbing her overstimulated clit was enough to get her off.

With a cry, she threw her head back, her orgasm spiraling up through her body. She felt a rush of hot fluid gush from her pussy, mixing with the cool water of the pool as she shook with the force of her orgasm. Captain Malone thrust several times quickly and then felt his hot load squirt into her as well, heard him grunt against her neck. She could feel every muscle in his body straining as he held himself in her, pushing her down, his fingers clutching her ass, his cock throbbing and pumping out the last of his load into her waiting pussy.

He held her a moment longer, both of them finally

relaxing as their orgasms faded. Ambiataqua slid her legs down Captain Malone's body. He held her gently as she found her footing on the bottom of the pool. She looked up into his dark eyes; as he leaned down to gently kiss her lips.

# CHAPTER 3

## CUNTS FROM OUTER SPACE

"THIS IS the Pluto Probe Ship. This is year five without fuel. We are adrift between the orbit of Pluto and Neptune, unable to accomplish our mission because an asteroid ruptured our fuel tank. Our only hope is someone or something rescues our crew of seven men. This is Captain Derek Sandion. We have sufficient food for only one more week. Chief Engineer Lonny Wen and I will remain conscious for that week. The ship is warm. Our communication system continues to function. Only a miracle will save us. Captain Derek Sandion out."

"In China, we say only the balance of Yin and Yang can save us."

Captain Sandion laughed. "That's got to be the best joke this entire trip, Wen. We were overbalanced from the start. Now we're going to die out of balance."

"I don't know about that," Engineer Wen said, "Things

always balance." He pressed a few buttons on the underside of a computer console on the deck of the helpless floating spaceship. "Return to engineering, Wen. And let me know when some pussy boards the ship."

Wen laughed. He was tall, a nice fellow. Always optimistic. Captain Sandion prevented himself from being optimistic. He relied on pragmatism or mysticism. Something needed to interfere with their present path. He didn't care how, or what, just as long as it was soon!

"Captain I think you'll want to see this."

"Put it on the main screen here." Captain Sandion ordered. "Coming on the screen now," said the chief engineer.

"What's that fog down there, Wen?" I can hardly see you. I only make out the main reactor core. It's not supposed to be purple is it?"

"No," Wen said. "That's a sign of a major system failure."

"It's going to knock our shields offline." Captain Scandion hurried to the shield panel. "We got to keep those asteroids from hitting us. We are flying enough miles per hour to breach our haul." "I'm trying to shut down part of the reactor."

"If you do that the men will come out of cryogenic animation." "Can't be helped, Sir."

"Go ahead. Do it, Wen." Captain Scandion switched the screen to the other decks of the ships. "It's on every floor, Wen."

"Reactor neutralized."

"Get to the lower deck and make sure the men are revived properly."

Captain Scandion switched back to engineering and saw Wen rushing out into the hall.

"This is Captain Scandion recording. The core reactor failed. Had to remove the other five crew members out of cryogenic animation. With only a day worth of food things don't look good. We encountered a strange fog all over the ship. The shields are back online but only at the expense of cryogenics being shut down."

Captain Scandion pulled out a photo of his wife, a lovely woman with green eyes and dark brown hair from Ukraine. "I'll miss you, Marvana."

Captain Scandion noticed a beautiful smell filling the atmosphere of the ship. At least I'll die with the smell of apricots and cucumbers. He lay back in his command chair, thinking of something to do when an oval object flashed overhead. It whizzed right by him. "What the fuck?"

He sat up and flipped the computer screen to several ship decks. "They're all over the place. Wen," Captain Scandion said over the intercom. "We've been invaded by some kind of Sea Crab creature."

"I can't move Captain." His voice sounded fearful. "They are all around us here in the cryogenic chambers.

Captain Scandion switched the main screen and

couldn't believe his eyes. His revived crew, five of them naked stood their back against the walls. Wen stood alongside them. Frozen.

"We can't move, Sir," said John. "They've got us."

"No one has got you!" Captain Scandion checked his laser gun. "I'm coming down there to free you."

"Don't do it, Sir," Wen said before his communication system failed.

Captain Scandion got up but was forced back down and held by the small oval creature. The flesh was soft and pink and reminded him of a sea crab. Only this creature flew. One landed on his right shoulder and now another left. Once they touched him, they broke away leaving little hickey marks on his naked skin.

"You're ready for mating," moaned the tiny creature. "Mating?"

Suddenly several of the creatures flew in through the air ducts. The elevator door suddenly popped open, allowing more to flood the deck of the Pluto Probe Ship. The creatures landed on Captain Scandion's eyes blinding him. One landed on his mouth and began to invade his tongue with flaps of wet flesh. Captain Scandion found himself behaving more cooperatively. He calmed down. Soon Captain Scandion found himself nude. All his clothes ripped off and each of the creatures took turns mounting him and fucking him. He wanted to yell, "Help," but instead he shouted, "Keep fucking me!"

. . .

When Captain Scandion came once spurting at his hot man seed down the creature's small gullet, the other creatures leaped from his eyes. They hovered over his eyes closely.

"You're floating--" he could hardly believe his own eyes. "Floating pussies!"

"You have been mated." The two hovering creatures said at the same time. "Things will improve. You will survive once we are born. We have been waiting for two thousand years for men to return to Pluto and Neptune's space."

Captain Scandion tried to focus, "Don't harm my men!"

After several days, Captain Scandion found himself surrounded by several pretty women of all races. All heights. All beautiful. Their leader called herself Cuntillisa.

"I shall repair your ship and upgrade it. You will be driven underground of Pluto and Neptune to reestablish our civilization. You have no control. It must be done."

"I'll do no such thing."

"Then you will die here aboard this ship once the male children are born in two days." "Ha. I'll be dead again before that without food." Captain Scandion countered haughtily.

"You should have died days ago. Only our blood kept you alive. Our vampire bites your shoulders. Now your food supplies flourish. We've upgraded your food replicators." "Damn you've cunts have thought of everything."

"We had plenty of time to think of everything," Cuntillisa said and smiled before straddling Captain Scandion's naked black thighs again. "Shall we fuck again?"

"I'm liking the way this is going." He paused. "Let me make one last computer entry. "Uh..." Captain Scandio looked at the long-haired blonde chick, her wavy blonde hair curled softly around her A-cup breasts and her thick inner pussy lips no longer floated without a body in space but between her gorgeous long legs. She had beautiful green eyes. "Everything seems to be all right now. We're going down to the planet. If you want to find us, bring the same amount of fuel and an all-male crew. Sign out Captain Scandion. Goddess Bless."

# CHAPTER 4

## ENDLESS BONER FUCKING

DURING MY JUNIOR year at Boston University, I went on Spring Break to Cancun, Mexico. Forget about the drug trade and all that nonsense. All I wanted was rest, relaxation and hot boys getting it on inside my even hotter pussy hole. So many handsome men were available, walking around shirtless and drunk. Naturally, my swim pants stayed wet and I never once entered the pool.

Also, my fingers stayed buried in my lily snatch all night. By morning, I smelled like a woman in heat for cock. I showered of course. And grudgingly I went out again for day four of Spring Break determined to get laid. This time I went out with my sorority girlfriends who were conducting a social experiment. They had this buff Android Robot about five feet six, had a chest like a boxer, thighs like a weight lifter, and the face of a runway model. What a face! Dark hair long enough to fall seductively over his blue eyes. Pink silicone skin covered the metal, so you didn't recognize right away he was all machine.

.   .   .

All the girls loved to hang around him and flirt. They drove those Cancun college girls crazy. Danny was the Android's name. He played cards. He could change a flat tire. He even knew how to repeat hot phrases those sorority girls planted in his brain database. Phrases like, "You need some hard and fast loving." Danny moved like a real human and the rumor was he fucks just as well as the next guy.

So we came back from bar hopping. I didn't get laid. I'm frustrated. It's late at night and Danny's giving me the flirty eyes sex stare. He opened his eyes wide and did not blink. A broad smile flowed across his face. He made his move and walked closer to me.

"I'm going to make you wet," Danny said, in a low masculine voice.

I was already wet. I started combing my long red hair with my hand and grinning. I pulled my hair down over the front of my shoulder, near my hard nubs. Nubs that stuck out a good one inch long, making an imprint in my blue stretch bra. Danny wore these distressed short jeans that left little to the imagination. He was hung. And I wanted to drop to my knees and suck his steel cock, but I needed to get Brittany's permission. Pretty Brittany was the senior in mechanical engineering. She also was president of her sorority.

Luckily, Brittany noticed Danny's interest in me.

"Slutty Lori, you've been slinking around in your blue

bra and bikini panties all night. No wonder Danny wants to stuff his fuel rod in your furnace."

"Brittany, I need more energy in my core reactor." All the sorority girls, Anna, Susan, and Lilja, laughed.

Brittany winked, "Don't worry, Lori. Danny always comes with an audience."


I've never fucked for an audience--not intentionally. I've never fucked a blue and silver Android either, although, in my science fiction reading, I've always wanted to. I decided to play the whore. I put on some disco music. I strutted and danced around Danny feeling up his massive chest. Rubbing my long warm fingers all over his silicone skin, I cooed. I touched ninety percent of his mechanical framework. His skin blushed a little when my hands rubbed across his manly beefcakes. I even weaved and draped my body all down his back, squatting lower and lower. My face lined up with his balls. I reached under his butt cheeks and pulled them back into my mouth. Danny flashed a lot of lights under the skin of his shin, as that's where his on-off circuitry was located.

"You keep warming my nuts and my semen's going to explode." Danny panted.

"I'll open wide and catch it all, Danny," I said, as I reached around from behind and started mauling his huge computer dick tool. He packed at least six inches and he was only warming up. I'd never had anyone over six inches. Maybe I was lucky. But maybe tonight, I'll lose my virginity a second time, too. I didn't think thoughts of love mattered. I didn't want them to matter. Danny was a machine after all. I'm sure Brittany had seen him naked before.

. . .

Brittany pulled out her statistical notebook and started recording Danny's reactions. Brittany said, "I've never seen Danny fuck. Who would have thought?"

Susan, Anna, and Lilija squealed, purred, and undressed out of their skimpy bar clothes. Most of the girls didn't wear panties. Our dubious idea centered on someone urging us into a wet T-shirt contest. And those sorority girls hated to lose at anything.

"Hey girls, Danny would make a great Biker." I cooed, "Just give him some fake tattoos all over his arms and chest."

"He is burly enough," Susan said, shamelessly rubbing her tits.

"I'll straddle him," said Lilija, after giving Anna a girly high-five. Both girls sat on the bed and spread their legs.


I had Danny's cock hard. I grabbed his slim hips and turned him around. My round-tit melons massaged his weightlifter thighs as he turned. His silicone skin even sweated a bit. His seven-inch cock nudged me in the left cheek. I steadied his mechanical dick tool. I opened my mouth wide and let my lips slide over the smooth real-like skin.

Danny moaned, "Suck that cock."

He moved down my gullet faster than a normal prick.

"He tastes better than a fake cock. He's got a cinnamon smell to his cranny hunter." The sorority girls squealed," Danny has a cinnamon cranny hunter!"

Overcome by lust, I shoved my other hand between my legs. My wet clit simmered in her juices. I relieved her by spreading the juices all around. Unable to control myself, I pulled my hand out of my juicy snatch and coated Danny's computerize-boner from base to helmet tip.

. . .

Danny humped his hips slowly at first inside my slippery hand. I pushed my hand back down toward my quivering twat. I opened wide for round two of blowjob sucking. My cheeks sucked in after I had Danny's seven inches in my wet mouth. My two fingers reached inside my heated core. My pussy furnace looked forward to meeting his steel horny cock.

Like a true cock hound, I never let his dick out of my sight.

He started to sweat. I jerked his cock, still in my mouth upward and gazed at his handsome face. His dark hair fell carelessly around his face and covered his eyes. He reached up and pushed his hair out of his face before gently pushing my long red hair out of the way.

When Danny asked, "Lori, will you love me, too?" My cunt exploded.

Brittany yelled, "Okay the sexperiment is over. No one is robbing me of the best decent cock I've had in twenty-one years."

She pushed me off Danny's saliva-drenched dick. Brittany squatted down and sucked him down in one swallow. "Yes, I will love you, Danny," Brittany replied.

All the sorority girls laughed. "Lori, you didn't think Danny was a virgin?"

I laughed, but I was disappointed too. I wanted to fuck Danny. Maybe I wanted to love him. What I decided was to take the same mechanical engineering class Brittany did. Next year, I'll take Danny for a sexperiment he's never had. I'll let him bang my asshole. Brittany hates ass sex. I'll finally find out what his Android jism feels like. But for now, I'm satisfied. I sucked Danny's Android cock. I can wait. After all, Brittany can't take Danny with her when she graduates this year.

# CHAPTER 5

## EROTIC JOURNEY TO
## THE MOON

AS LIEUTENANT AMANDA SANDERS stepped into the Genesis spacecraft for the first time, the first thing that caught her attention was Captain Mason Catani. He was the handsome man who had successfully commanded the spacecraft on its various missions out of space for the last decade. Captain Catani and Amanda did have some history together. They had actually been high school sweethearts who lost contact when they went to college. Now that she had met him again, she intended to never let him go.

Their mission was the moon. And the crew seemed overly excited. After the briefing, the shuttle took off and everyone settled into their various quarters. As Amanda took her shower, she was elated when the captain visited her while she took her shower.

"Why don't you join me captain?" she teased. When he did, she was startled. She'd tried to talk to him, but he'd put a finger to her lips and refused to speak.

As they stood beneath the hot water, he'd pulled her against his hard body, his hands running down her back to cup her ass, as his mouth descended on hers. He pressed his erection against her stomach, slowly rubbing it back and forth. She could feel the hot slickness of it against her skin. His tongue was hot as it ran over her lips, forcing her mouth open. She wound her arms around his neck, pressing her wet breasts against his chest.

Mason's hands were moving further, spreading her ass with his hands, fingers probing between the backs of her thighs. He was thrusting his cock against her stomach with some force now and she suspected he wanted to have sex standing up in the shower. At times, he enjoyed positions that kept her off balance and kept him in complete control. This was apparently one of those times.

Before Mason could react, Amanda reached behind him for the safety railing that ran around the wall of the shower, pulling herself against him, pinning him to the wall with her body. He broke their kiss, looking down at her in surprise. He opened his mouth to speak, but she placed a silencing finger on his lips.

Amanda slowly slid one leg up Mason's body, over his hip, her foot resting at the small of his back, opening her to Mason. She let go of the railing long enough to guide Mason's hard cock to her opening, sliding the tip into her sex. Mason was apparently over his confusion at losing control of the situation and held Amanda's leg, supporting her weight. He thrust upward slowly as Amanda pulled herself against him, using the rail as leverage. She looked up at him, his eyes dark with passion. She held him there, fully inside of her, feeling his length as she settled her weight on him. It was an amazing sensation to have his cock sheathed inside her; he was so long that he filled her completely. She could stay like this forever. Mason tilted her chin up to look into her eyes. He cocked an eyebrow at her and said one word, "Dinner."

The meaning was clear; they did not have much time. He began rocking his hips, thrusting himself even further into Amanda. She gasped with each stroke, using the rail to pull herself against him, matching each of his thrusts. Mason had let go of her ass, moving his hand to her breast, looking down as he fondled her. She watched him as he looked past her breasts, looking down to watch his cock sliding in and out of her pussy. She saw his lips part, heard his sharp intake of breath.

His thrusting grew harder and faster; he tipped his head back, eyes closed. Amanda wondered for the hundredth time what was going on in his head. But the thought left her mind as the sensations in her body took over.

She adjusted her balance as Mason pulled her leg higher, giving him more access but almost lifting her from the tile, her foot sliding on the slick floor. He was holding her ass again, pushing her down against his thrusts, grunting with each stroke, close to his orgasm. Amanda wasn't close to coming but she sensed for some reason Mason needed this more than she did right now. Amanda leaned into Mason's chest. He wrapped his arms tightly around her, holding her against him as he thrust his hips frantically, seeking his release. Amanda nuzzled his neck, running her tongue up to his ear, flicking his earlobe, and then sucking on it gently. As she expected, the extra sensation was enough to send him over the edge.

He bucked up suddenly, almost toppling them both, a hoarse cry more pain than pleasure coming from deep in his chest. Amanda held on to the railing, riding out his climax as he thrust almost violently into her several more times, his cock shooting load after hot load into her. She felt him finally shudder against her, his head dropping to her shoulder, his breathing ragged.

He let go of her leg and she slumped against his chest. He held her against him, gently swaying back and forth, as his orgasm faded and his breathing returned to normal. He kissed her tenderly on her eyes and lips.

"Sorry, babe. You didn't come, did you? I'll make it up to you." He kissed her once more and turned her toward the shower. "We need to get you clean for dinner." He grabbed the bath soap, lathering his hands, running them over her body, soaping her breasts, and running his hands between her legs. He let the water rinse away the sweet-smelling soap before kneeling down in front of Amanda. He spread the lips of her pussy, running his tongue over her swollen clit.

Amanda was still highly aroused from their lovemaking and at his touch; she slumped against the shower wall, her knees weak. She grabbed the rail behind her to keep from sliding to the floor.

Mason knew his tongue on her clit was the fastest way to make her come. She held his head as he licked her, sucking her clit like he sucked on her nipples. She began to cry out, her hips pushing forward, seeking release.

She came violently, her back arching, twisting, and grinding against Mason's face. He kept licking, sucking at her, seemingly unable to stop until she pushed his head away. She slid down the wall, the water pounding on her, Mason kneeling on the shower floor. He reached out and pulled her into his lap, holding her as her breathing slowed and she returned to a more or less normal state.

"I think we're even," she finally found her voice. "That was incredible."

"I know." He gave her a cocky grin. "And now, we've reacquainted ourselves," he smiled.

Amanda smiled knowing that her first trip to the moon would be one hell of an adventure.

# ABOUT THE AUTHOR

Helana Parkins is an emerging erotica author of many erotica kinks and sub-genres. Be sure to check out other books and leave a review if this story got you hot!

Visit my blog at Helana Parkins Blog

Join my newsletter for exclusive previews Helana Parkins Newsletter

Sign up for Free Stories from Xplicit Press Authors

Xplicit Press Author Updates

Like Xplicit Press on Facebook

Follow Xplicit Press on Twitter

Readers: I want to expand a few of the stories to see where the characters can be explored further. If there are any of the stories that you would like to read more about again, I'd love to hear from you!

*Keep In Touch*
Helana Parkins
info@helanaparkins.com